THE TRAVELING CHILD GOES TO
Rio de Janeiro

Written By:
Monet Hambrick

ISBN 978-1-7330082-0-4

For my daughters Jordyn and Kennedy who constantly push me to be better than I was yesterday. –MH

It was spring break, and we were so excited our family was going to Rio de Janeiro. Our parents told us it's in the country of Brazil, which is the biggest country on the continent of South America.

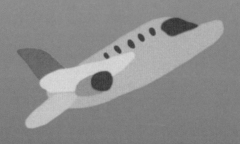

Today was the day we were going to the airport to go on our trip. Our parents packed coloring books, snacks, headphones, and toys for us to entertain ourselves on the plane.

They packed all of these things, but our favorite part was getting to watch all the free kids movies.

After a long nap, we woke up right when our plane landed. We were finally in Rio de Janeiro! "Ola!" the flight attendant said, and told us that is how to say hello in Portuguese. It's the language spoken in Brazil.

Our parents grabbed our bags, and we walked off the plane. We thought we would go right outside, but we had to stand in a line to get our passports stamped.

It was finally time to explore. We went to see the Christ the Redeemer statue. Our mommy said it's one of the Seven Wonders of the World!

It's on top of a really big mountain, so we took a cool train to get close. Our daddy showed us a picture of the statue and told us it was 125 feet tall. But, wow, when we saw it, it was huge!

The next day we went to a futebol match. It's the biggest sport in Brazil. Daddy said we call it soccer in the United States.

The match was in Maracanã Stadium, where the 2016 Olympic Games were held. How cool is that? We quickly joined the cheering crowd, rooting for the home team!

We love to dance, and before we came to Rio de Janeiro, our mommy told us the Afro-Brazilians invented a dance called samba.

We had the time of our lives moving to the African-inspired beats of samba music. Watch out school talent show—we're ready for you!

Our family loves enjoying the outdoors, so our parents took us on the coolest hike to Pedra do Telégrafo. We had to walk through the trees and climb up some rocks.

We slowed our parents down just a little, but luckily they didn't mind. When we made it to the top, we saw the prettiest view ever.

We love to eat, and on our first night we tried Brazil's traditional dish Moqueca fish. Since we like helping in the kitchen, we all took a cooking class to learn how to make it.

Now we can help our parents cook it at home!

Okay, we'll admit, when our parents told us we were going to Jardim Botanico, the botanical gardens in Rio de Janeiro, we weren't that thrilled. Who wants to see a bunch of trees?

When we got there we saw way more than trees, there were monkeys running all around. We even saw funny shaped cacti, called corkscrew cacti!

Our tour guide kept telling us about this beautiful staircase, Escadaria Selaron. He said it was made out of colorful tiles, and we just had to see it.

When we got there, we learned it took twenty-three years to complete. Wow, that's way older than us!

Sadly, it was time to go home. We had so much fun exploring Rio de Janeiro. We can't wait for our next adventure!

Made in the USA
Columbia, SC
16 December 2019